THE
LAYERS

A
Short
Novel
from
Astounding
Stories

EVERETT B.
COLE

THE PLAYERS

A Playboy is someone with power, too much time on his hands, and too little sense of a goal worth achieving. And if the Playboy happens to belong to a highly advanced culture....

Illustrated by Solo

THE PLAYERS

EVERETT B. COLE

WILDSIDE PRESS

THE PLAYERS

Originally published in *Astounding Science Fiction* April 1955. Copyright not renewed.

THE PLAYERS

Through the narrow streets leading to the great plaza of Karth, swarmed a colorful crowd — buyers, idlers, herdsmen, artisans, traders. From all directions they came, some to gather around the fountain, some to explore the wineshops, many to examine the wares, or to buy from the merchants whose booths and tents hid the cobblestones.

A caravan wound its way through a gate and stopped, the weary beasts standing patiently as the traders sought vacant space where they might open business. From another gate, a herdsman guided his living wares through the crowd, his working animals snapping at the heels of the flock, keeping it together and in motion.

Musa, trader of Karth, sat cross-legged before his shop, watching the scene with quiet amusement. Business was good in the city, and his was pleasingly above the average. Western caravans had come in, exchanging their goods for those eastern wares he had acquired. Buyers from the city and from the surrounding hills had come to him, to exchange their coin for his goods. He glanced back into the booth, satisfied with what he saw, then resumed his casual watch of the plaza. No one seemed interested in him.

There were customers in plenty. Men stopped, critically examined the contents of the displays, then moved on, or stayed to bargain. One of these paused before Musa, his eyes dwelling on the merchant rather than on his wares.

The shopper was a man of medium height. His rather slender, finely featured face belied the apparent heaviness of his body, though his appearance was not actually abnormal. Rather, he gave the impression of being a man of powerful physique and ascetic habits. His dress was that of a herdsman, or possibly of an owner of herds from the northern Galankar.

Musa arose, to face him.

"Some sleeping rugs, perhaps? Or a finely worked bronze jar from the East?"

The stranger nodded. "Possibly. But I would like to look a while if I may."

Musa stepped aside, waving a hand. "You are more than welcome, friend," he assented. "Perhaps some of my poor goods may strike your fancy."

"Thank you." The stranger moved inside.

Musa stood at the entrance, watching him. As the man stepped from place to place, Musa noted that he seemed to radiate a certain confidence. There was a definite aura of power and ability. This man, the trader decided, was no ordinary herdsman. He commanded more than sheep.

"You own herds to the North?" he asked.

The stranger turned, smiling. "Lanko is my name," he said. "Yes, I come from the North." He swept a hand to indicate the merchandise on display, and directed a questioning gaze at the merchant. "It seems strange that your goods are all of the East. I see little of the West in all your shop."

*****

Normally, Musa kept his own council, assuming that his affairs were not public property, but his alone. There was something about this man, Lanko, however, which influenced him to break his usual reticence.

"I plan a trading trip to the Eastern Sea," he confided. "Of course, to carry eastern goods again to the East would be a waste of time, so I am reserving my western goods for the caravan and clearing out the things of the East."

Lanko nodded. "I see." He pointed to a small case of finely worked jewelry. "What would be the price of those earrings?"

Musa reached into the case, taking out a cunningly worked pair of shell and gold trinkets.

"These are from Norlar, a type of jewelry we rarely see here," he said. "For these, I must ask twenty balata."

Lanko whistled softly. "No wonder you would make a

6

trip East. I wager there is profit in those." He pointed. "What of the sword up there?"

Musa laughed. "You hesitate at twenty balata, then you point out that?"

He crossed the tent, taking the sword from the wall. Drawing it from its scabbard, he pointed to the unusually long, slender blade.

"This comes from Norlar, too. But the smith who made it is still farther to the east, beyond the Great Sea." He gripped the blade, flexing it.

"Look you," he commanded, "how this blade has life. Here is none of your soft bronze or rough iron from the northern hills. Here is a living metal that will sever a hair, yet not shatter on the hardest helm."

Lanko showed interest. "You say this sword was made beyond the Great Sea? How, then, came it to Norlar and thence here?"

Musa shook his head. "I am not sure," he confessed. "It is rumored that the priests of the sea god, Kondaro, by praying to their deity, are guided across the sea to lands unknown."

"Taking traders with them?"

"So I have been told."

"And you plan to journey to Norlar to verify this rumor, and perhaps to make a sea voyage?"

Musa stroked his beard, wondering if this man could actually read thoughts.

"Yes," he admitted, "I had that in mind."

"I see." Lanko reached for the sword. As Musa handed it to him, he extended it toward the rear of the booth, whipping it in an intricate saber drill. Musa watched, puzzled. An experienced swordsman himself he had thought he knew all of the sword arts. The sword flexed, singing as it cut through the air.

"Merchant, I like this sword. What would its price be?"

*****

Musa was disappointed. Here was strange bargaining.

7

People just didn't walk in and announce their desire for definite articles. They feigned indifference. They picked over the wares casually, disparagingly. They looked at many items, asking prices. They bargained a little, perhaps, to test the merchant. They made comments about robbery, and about the things they had seen in other merchants' booths which were so much better and so much cheaper.

Slowly, and with the greatest reluctance, did the normal shopper approach the object he coveted.

Then, here was this man.

"*Well*," Musa told himself, "*make the most of it*." He shrugged.

"Nine hundred balata," he stated definitely, matching the frank directness of this unusual shopper, and incidentally doubling his price.

Lanko was examining the hilt of the sword. He snapped a fingernail against its blade. There was a musical *ping*.

"You must like this bit of metal far better than I," he commented without looking up. "I only like it two hundred balata worth."

Musa felt relief at this return to familiar procedure. He held up his hands in a horrified gesture.

"Two hundred!" he cried. "Why, that is for the craftsman's apprentices. There is yet the master smith, and those who bring the weapon to you. No, friend, if you want this prince of swords, you must expect to pay for it. One does not — " He paused. Lanko was sheathing the weapon, his whole bearing expressing unwilling relinquishment.

Musa slowed his speech. "Still," he said softly, "I am closing out my eastern stock, after all. Suppose we make it eight hundred fifty?"

"Did you say two hundred fifty?" Lanko held the sheathed sword up, turning to the light to inspect the leather work.

The bargaining went on. Outside, the crowds in the street thinned, as the populace started for their evening meals. The sword was inspected and re-inspected. It slid out of its sheath and back again. Finally, Musa sighed.

"Well, all right. Make it five hundred, and I'll go to dinner with you." He shook his head in a nearly perfect imitation of despair. "May the wineshop do better than I did."

*****

"Housewife, this is Watchdog. Over."

The man at the workbench looked around. Then, he laid his tools aside, and picked up a small microphone.

"This is Housewife," he announced.

"Coming in."

The worker clipped the microphone to his jacket, and crossed the room to a small panel. He threw a switch, looked briefly at a viewscreen, then snapped another switch.

"Screen's down," he reported. "Come on in, Lanko."

An opening appeared in the wall, to show a fleeting view of a bleak landscape. Bare rocks jutted from the ice, kept clear of snow by the shrieking wind. Extreme cold crept into the room, then a man swept in and the wall resumed its solidity behind him.

He stood for an instant, glancing around, then shrugged off a light robe and started shedding equipment.

"Hi, Pal," he was greeted. "How are things down Karth way?"

"Nothing exceptional." Lanko shrugged. "This area's getting so peaceful it's monotonous." He unsnapped his accumulator and crossed to the power generator.

"No wars, or rumors of wars," he continued. "The town's getting moral — very moral, and it's developing into a major center of commerce in the process." He kicked off his sandals, wriggled out of the baggy native trousers, and tossed his shirt on top of them.

"No more shakedowns. Tax system's working the way it was originally intended to, and the merchants are flocking in."

He walked toward the wall, flicking a hand out. An

9

opening appeared, and he ducked through it.

"Be with you in a minute, Banasel," he called over his shoulder. "Like to get cleaned up."

Banasel nodded and went back to the workbench. He picked up a small part, examined it, touched it gently a few times with a soft brush, and replaced it in the device he was working on.

He tightened it into place, and was checking another component when a slight shuffle announced his companion's return.

"Oh, yes," said Lanko. "Met your old pal, Musa. He's doing right well for himself."

Banasel swung around. "Haven't seen him since we joined the Corps. What's he doing?"

"Trading." Lanko opened a locker, glancing critically at the clothing within. "He set up shop with the load of goods we gave him long ago, and did some pretty shrewd merchandising. Now, he's planning a trip over the Eastern Sea. He hinted at a rumor of a civilization out past Norlar."

"Nothing out there for several thousand kilos," growled Banasel, "except for a few little islands." He jerked a thumb toward the workbench. "I can't show you right now, because the scanner's down for cleaning, but there isn't even an island for the first couple thousand K's. Currents are all wrong, too. No one could cross without navigational equipment."

"I know," Lanko assured him. "We haven't checked over that way for a long time, but I still remember. I didn't put it exactly that way, of course, but I did ask Musa how he planned to get over the Eastern. And, I got an answer." He paused as he gathered up the garments he had discarded.

"It seems there's a new priesthood at Norlar, who've got something," he continued. "It's all wrapped up in religious symbology, and they don't let any details get out, but they are guiding ships out to sea, and they're bringing them back again, loaded with goods that never originated in

the Galankar, or in any place accessible to the Galankar."
He hung up the last article of clothing and turned, a
sheathed sword in his hand.

"Musa sold me this," he said, extending the hilt toward
Banasel. "I never saw anything like it on this planet. Did
you?"

*****

Banasel accepted the weapon, drawing it from its
scabbard. He examined the handwork on the hilt, then
snapped a fingernail against the blade. As he listened to the
musical *ping*, the technician looked at the weapon with
more interest. Gently, he flexed it, watching for signs of
strain. Lanko grinned at him.

"Go ahead," he invited, "get rough with it. That's a
sword you're holding, Chum, not one of those bronze skull
busters."

Banasel extended the sword, whipping it violently. The
blade bent, then straightened, and bent again, as it slashed
through the air.

"Well," he murmured. "Something new."

He put the sword on the workbench and took an
instrument from a cabinet. For a few minutes, he busied
himself taking readings and tapping out data on his
computer. He sat back, looking at the sword curiously. At
last, he glanced at the computer, then put the test
instrument he had been using back in the cabinet, taking
another to replace it. After taking more readings, he looked
at the computer, then shook his head, turning to Lanko.

"This," he said slowly, "is excellent steel. Of course, it
could be an accidental alloy, but I wouldn't think anyone
on this planet could have developed the technology to get it
just so." He held the sword away from him, looking at it
closely. "Assuming an accidental alloy, an accident in
getting precisely the right degree of heat before quenching,
and someone who ground and polished with such care as to
leave the temper undisturbed, while getting this finish —
Oh, it's possible, all right. But 'tain't likely. Musa told you

11

this came from overseas?"

"To the best of his knowledge. He got it from a trader who claimed to have been on a voyage across the Eastern Sea."

Banasel leaned back, clasping his hands behind his head. "You must have had quite a talk with Musa. Did he remember you?"

Lanko shook his head. "Don't be foolish," he grunted. "You and I were blotted out of his memory, remember? So are quite a few of the things that happened around Atakar, way back when. He's got a complete past, of course, but we're not part of it.

"No, he had a booth in the Karth market. I came through, just looking things over, and recognized him. So, I picked an acquaintance. Beat him down to about half the asking price for this sword, still leaving him a whopping profit. He went to dinner with me, still bewailing the rooking I'd given him. Told you, he's a trader. We had quite a talk, certainly. But we were strangers."

"Yeah." Banasel looked off into space. "Seems funny. You and I were born on this planet. We were brought up here, and a lot of people once knew us. But they've all forgotten, and we don't belong any more. I'm beginning to see what they mean by 'the lonely life of a guardsman.'"

He was silent for a time, then looked at his companion.

"Do you think these priests at Norlar might be in our line of business?"

"Could be," nodded Lanko. "There's a lot of seafaring out of Konassa, and there are several other busy seaports we know of. But no one in any of them ever heard of navigation out of sight of land, let alone trying it. There's nothing but pilotage, and even that's pretty sketchy. And, there's this thing." He crossed to the workbench, picked up the sword, and stroked its blade.

"Normally," he mused, "technical knowledge gets around. Part of it's developed here, part there. Then someone comes along and puts it together. And someone else adds to it. And so on.

"Then, there are other times, when there's an abnormal source, or where there are unusual conditions, and knowledge is very closely guarded. This might be one of those cases, and those priests might be fronting for someone very much in our line of business." He broke off.

"Any maedli hot?"

"Sure." Banasel picked a pot from the heater and poured two cups.

"Think we should set up a base near Norlar and have a look?"

"Probably be a good idea." Lanko accepted a cup, took a sip, and shook his head violently.

"Ouch! I said hot, not boiling." He blew on the cup and set it aside to steam itself cool.

"These mountains were an excellent base," he continued, "but this area seems to be developing perfectly. There's no outside interference, all traces of former interference have been eliminated, and there's very little excuse for us to hang around." He picked up the cup again, cautiously sampling its contents. "And it's about time we moved around and checked on the rest of the planet."

Banasel turned back to the workbench. "Good idea," he agreed. "I'll get this scanner set up again, and we'll be ready to load out." He picked up his tools. "As I remember, Norlar has a mountainous backbone where no one ever goes. We should be able to set up right on the island."

*****

On the eastern slope of the Midra Kran, a cloud of dust paced a caravan, which wound up the trail, through a pass. The treachery of the narrow path was testified to by an occasional slither, followed by a startled curse.

Musa stood in his stirrups, looking ahead at the long trail which twisted a little farther up, then dropped to the wide Jogurthan plateau. Far ahead, over the poorly marked way, he knew, was another range, the Soruna Kran, which blocked his way to the Eastern Sea.

He looked back at the straggling caravan.

"Better get them to close up, Baro," he remarked. "We'd be in a lot of trouble if a robber band caught us scattered like this."

The other trader nodded and turned his mount. Then, he paused as shouts came from the rear of the line. Mixed with the shouting was the clatter of weapons.

"Come on," cried Musa. "It's happened."

He kicked his mount in the ribs, and swung about, starting up the steep bank. The bandits would have bowmen posted to deal with anyone who might try to get back along the narrow path, and he had no desire to test the accuracy of their aim.

As his beast scrambled up the bank, Musa saw a man standing on a pinnacle, alertly watching the center of the caravan. His guess had been right. The bandit leader's strategy had been to cut the caravan in two, and to deal with the rear guard first. As the watcher started to aim at something down on the trail, Musa quickly raised his own bow and sent an arrow to cut the man down before he could fire.

It was a good shot. The man made no sound as the arrow struck, but clawed for an instant at the shaft in his side, then dropped, to slide down the face of a low cliff. Musa, followed by his guards, stormed up the slope.

They went through a saddle in the hill, to find themselves confronted by a half dozen men, who swung about, trying to bring their bows to bear on the unexpected targets. Two of these went down as arrows sang through the air, then the traders were upon the rest, swords flailing, too close for archery.

One of the bandits swung his sword wildly at Musa, who had drawn a twin to that blade he had sold back in Karth. The slender shaft of steel rang against the bandit's bronze blade, deflecting it, then Musa made a quick thrust which passed through the man's leather shield, to penetrate flesh. The bronze weapon sagged, and its holder staggered.

14

Musa jerked back violently, disengaged his sword, and made a swift cut. For an instant, the bandit sat his mount, staring at his opponent. Then, he slumped, and rolled loosely from his saddle.

The action had been fast. Only one bandit, a skilled swordsman, remained, to keep Baro busy. Musa rode quickly behind him, thrusting as he passed. Baro looked across the limp body.

"Now, what did you have to do that for?" he demanded. "I was having a good time."

"Let's get down to the trail again," Musa told him. "We can have a wonderful time there." He pointed.

The caravan's rear guard was in trouble. Several of them were in the dust of the trail, and the survivors were being pressed by a number of determined swordsmen.

Baro wheeled and slid down the incline, closely followed by the rest of the group.

The surrounded bandits fought desperately, but hopelessly. The charge from the hill had driven them off balance, and they were never given a chance to recover. At last, Musa and Baro looked over the results of the raid.

They had lost several guards. One trader, Klaron, had been killed by an arrow launched early in the attack. Several of the survivors were wounded.

"We'll have to hire some more guards and drivers in Jogurth," said Baro. "And what are we going to do about Klaron's goods?"

"We can divide them and sell them in Jogurth," Musa told him. "Klaron has a brother back in Karth who can use the money, and money's a lot easier to carry than goods. You'll see him on your return trip."

Baro nodded, and started up the line, reorganizing the caravan. At last, they got under way again, and resumed their slow way toward the plateau.

*****

The caravan went on, to enter the plateau, where the traders started resting by day and traveling by night, to avoid exertion during the day's heat.

They came to the city of Jogurth, which for most of them was a terminal. From there, they would return to Karth, a few possibly going on to their homes still farther west. Musa stayed in town for a few days, trading his few remaining eastern goods for locally produced articles, and helping in the sale of Klaron's goods. At last, he joined another caravan, headed by an old trader, Kerunar, who habitually traveled between Jogurth and Manotro, on the east coast.

The trip across the Soruna Kran was uneventful, and Musa finally saw the glint of the Eastern Sea. He did not stay long in Manotro, for he discovered that the small channel ships traveled frequently, and he was able to guide his pack beasts to the wharf, where his bales were accepted for shipment. Leaving his goods, he led his animals back to the market.

Old Kerunar shook his head when he saw Musa. "Be careful, son," he cautioned. "I've been coming here for twenty years. Used to trade in Norlar, too. But you couldn't get me over there now for ten thousand caldor."

"Oh?" Musa looked at him curiously. "What's wrong?"

Kerunar looked at his newly set up booth. Hung about it were durable goods and trinkets from a dozen cities. There were articles even from far-off Telon, in the Konassan gulf. He looked back at Musa.

"Norlar," he declared, "has fallen into the hands of thieves and murderers. You can trade there, to be sure. You can even make a profit. But you cannot be sure you will not excite the avarice of the Kondarans, or arouse their anger. For they have a multitude of strange laws, which they can invoke against anyone, and which they enforce with confiscation of goods. Death or slavery await any who protest their actions or question their rules." He paused.

"Some manage to trade, and come back with profitable bales. Some leave their goods in the hands of the priests of Kondaro. Some remain, to find a quick death. But I stop here. I prefer to deal with honorable men. When I face the thief or the bandit, I prefer to have a weapon in my hand. A book of strange laws can be worse than any bandit born."

Musa looked about the market. "Here, of course," he acknowledged, "are the goods of the Far East. But I must see them at their source." He shook his head. "No," he decided, "I shall make one trip at least."

"I'll give you just one word of caution, then," he was told. "Whatever you see, make little comment. Whenever you are asked for an offering, make no objection, but give liberally. Keep your eyes open and your opinions to yourself."

"Thanks." Musa grinned. "I'll try to remember."

"Don't just remember. Follow the advice, if you wish to

return."

Musa's grin widened. "I'll be back," he promised.

*****

The harbor of Tanagor, chief seaport of Norlar, was full of shipping. Here were the ships which plied the trackless wastes of the Eastern Sea. Huge, red-sailed, broad-beamed, they rode at anchor in the harbor, served by small galleys from the city. Tied up at the wharves, were the smaller, yellow and white-sailed ships which crossed the channel between the mainland and the island empire.

Slowly, Musa's ship drew in toward the wharf, where a shouting gang of porters and stevedores awaited her arrival. Together with other passengers, Musa stood at the rail, watching the activity on the pier.

Four slaves, bearing a crimson curtained litter, came to the wharf and stopped. The curtains opened, and a man stepped out. He was not large, nor did his face or figure differ from the normal. But his elegantly embroidered crimson and gold robes made him a colorfully outstanding figure, even on this colorful waterfront. And the imperious assurance of his bearing made him impossible to ignore.

He adjusted his strangely shaped, flat cap, glanced about the wharf haughtily, and beckoned to one of the slaves, who reached inside the litter and took from it an ornately decorated crimson chest. Another slave joined him, and the two, carrying the chest with every evidence of reverent care, followed their crimson-cloaked master as he strode into a pier office.

Musa turned to one of the other merchants, his eyebrows raised inquiringly.

"A priest of Kondaro," whispered the other. "In this land, they are supreme. Take care never to anger one of them, or to approach too closely to the sacred chest their slaves carry. To do so can mean prompt execution."

As Musa started to thank the man for his friendly warning, a cry of "Line Ho!" caused him to turn his attention to the mooring parties. Lines had been cast aboard at bow and stern, and the ship was rapidly being secured to stout bollards ashore.

A gang of stevedores quickly rigged a gangway amidships, and porters commenced streaming aboard to carry the cargo ashore. Another gangway was rigged aft for the passengers. At the foot of this, stood one of the priest's litter bearers, a slave with a crimson loincloth. In his hands, he held a large, red bowl, which was decorated with intricate gold designs. Beside him, stood his companion, a sturdy, frowning fellow, who held a large, strangely shaped sword in his hand. Musa's previous mentor leaned toward him nodding to the group.

"Don't forget or fail to put a coin in that bowl," he cautioned. "Otherwise, you'll never get passage on one of the sacred ships."

"How much?" queried Musa.

"The more, the better. If you want quick passage across the Great Sea, better make it at least ten caldor."

Musa shrugged, reaching into his purse for a gold coin.

"Maybe I should be in the priesthood myself, instead of the trading business," he told himself silently.

As he passed the bowl, he noted that the other trader dropped only a silver piece. On the wharf, the incoming passengers were being guided into groups. Musa noted that his group was the smallest, and that his previous friend had gone to another, larger group. An official, tablet in hand, approached.

"Your name, Traveler?"

"Musa, trader, of Karth."

"You have goods?"

"I brought twelve bales. They are marked with my name."

"Very good, sir. We will hold them for your disposal. You may claim them at any time after mid-day." The man wrote rapidly on his tablet.

Musa thanked him, then turned to see how his shipboard acquaintance was progressing. He had questions to ask about gold and silver coins.

He watched the older merchant complete his conversation with an official, and, as he started to leave the wharf, quickly caught up with him. At Musa's approach, the other held up a hand.

"I know," he said. "Why did I tell you to make a generous offering, then put a smaller coin in the bowl myself? That is what you want to know?"

"Precisely," Musa replied. "I'm not a poor man, but I'm not a wealthy holiday seeker, either. This voyage has to pay."

The other smiled. "Exactly why I advised you as I did. Come into this wineshop, and I'll tell you the story."

*****

Over the drinks, the older man explained himself. An experienced trader, he had been operating between the mainland and Norlar for many years. It had been a profitable business, for the island had been dependent upon the mainland for many staple items, and had in return furnished many items of exquisite craftsmanship, as well as the produce of its extensive fisheries and pearl beds.

Then, the prophet, Sira Nal, had come with his preachings of a great sea god, Kondaro, ruler of the Eastern Sea. Tonda told of the unbelief that had confronted the prophet, and of the positive proof that Sira Nal had offered, when he had gathered a group of converts, collected enough money to purchase a ship, and made a highly successful voyage to the distant lands to the east. Upon his return, Sira Nal had found a ready market for the strange and wonderful products he had brought. He also had found many more converts for his new religion.

His original group, now a priesthood, were the only men who could give protection and guidance to a ship in a voyage past the sea demons who frequented the Eastern Sea, and they demanded large offerings to compensate for their services. Of course, a few adventurous shipowners had attempted to duplicate Sira Nal's feat without the aid of a priest, but no living man had seen their ships or crews again.

The profits from the rich, new trade, plus the alms of the traders visiting Tanagor, had rapidly filled the coffers of Kondaro. A great temple had been built, and the priests had become more and more powerful, until now, not too many years after the first voyage of Sira Nal, they virtually ruled the island.

For some years, Tonda, a conservative man and a firm believer in his own ancestral gods, had paid little attention to this strange, new religion. Upon arrival at Tanagor, to be sure, he had sometimes placed small offerings in the votive bowl, but more often, he had merely strode past the Slave of Kondaro, and gone upon his affairs.

At last, however, attracted by the great profits in the new, oversea trade, he had decided to arrange for a voyage in one of the great ships. Then, the efficiency of the priestly bookkeeping methods had become apparent. The Great God had become incensed at Tonda's impiety during his many previous trips across the channel, and a curse had been placed upon him and upon his goods. Of course, if Tonda wished to do penance, and to make votive offerings, amounting to about two thousand caldor, it might be that the Great God would relent and allow his passage, but only with new goods. His former possessions had been destroyed by the angry Kondaro in his wrath at Tonda's attempts to place them in one of the sacred ships. Empty-handed, Tonda had returned to the mainland.

"But why did you return with more goods?" inquired Musa.

Tonda smiled. "The wrath of Kondaro extends only to the Great Sea. And, even though I cannot go farther east, trade here in Tanagor is quite profitable." He paused, smiling, as he sipped his drink.

"I think the priests like having a few penitents around to explain things to newcomers, and to furnish examples of the power of Kondaro."

Musa smiled in response. "But my ten caldor make me and my goods acceptable?"

Tonda looked around quickly, then turned a horrified face toward his protégé.

"Never say such things," he cautioned in a low tone of voice. "Don't even think them. Your piety makes you acceptable, so long as you continue in a way pleasing to the great Kondaro. The money means nothing. It is only the spirit of sacrifice that counts."

"I see." Musa's face was solemn. "And how else may I be sure I will remain acceptable?"

Tonda nodded approvingly. "I thought you were a man of good sense and prudence." He launched into a description of the technicalities of the worship of Kondaro, the god of the Eastern Sea.

At length, Musa left his tutor, and repaired to an inn, where he secured lodging for the night.

*****

The following morning, in obedience to the advice given him by Tonda, Musa took his way toward the Temple of the Sea. As he threaded through the crowds already gathering in the streets, he took note of the types of merchandise displayed in the booths, and hawked by the street peddlers. Suddenly, one of these roving sellers approached him. In his hands he held a number of ornaments.

"Good day to you, oh Traveler," he cried. "Surely, it is a fortunate morning for both of us." With a deft gesture, he threw one of the trinkets, a cunningly contrived amulet, about Musa's neck.

Musa would have brushed the man aside, but the chain of the amulet had tangled about his neck and he was forced to pause while removing it.

"I told myself when I saw you," the man continued, "ah, Banasel, here is one who should be favored by the gods. Now, how can such a one venture upon the Eastern Sea without a sacred amulet?"

22

Musa had slipped the chain over his head. He paused, holding the ornament in his hand. "How, then, are you to know where I am going?"

"Oh, Illustrious Traveler," exclaimed the man, "how can I fail to know these things when it is given to me to vend these amulets of great fortune?"

In spite of himself, Musa was curious. He looked at the amulet. There was no question as to the superb workmanship, and his trading instincts took over.

"Why, this is a fair piece of work," he said. "Possibly I could spare a caldor or so."

The man before him struck his forehead.

"A caldor, he says! Why, the gold alone is worth ten."

Musa looked more closely at the ornament. The man was probably not exaggerating too much. Actually, he knew he could get an easy twenty-five balata for the bauble in Karth. A rapid calculation told him that here was a possible profit from the skies.

"Why, possibly it is worth five, at that," he said. "Look, I'll be generous. Shall we say six?"

"Oh, prince of givers! Thou paragon of generosity! After all, I, too, must live." The man smiled wryly. "However, you are a fine, upstanding young man, and one must make allowance. I had thought to ask twenty, but we'll make it ten. Just the price of the gold."

Musa smiled inwardly. The profit was secured, but maybe —

"Let's make it eight, and I'll give you my blessing with the money."

The man held out his hand. "Nine."

Musa shrugged. "Very well, most expert of vendors." He reached into his purse.

*****

Banasel hesitated before accepting the money. He looked Musa over carefully, then nodded as if satisfied.

"Yes," he said softly, "I was right." He paused, then addressed himself directly to Musa.

23

"We must be very careful to whom we sell these enchanted amulets," he explained, "for they are talismans of the greatest of powers. The wearer of one of these need never fear the unjust wrath of man, beast, or demon, for he has powerful protectors at his call. Only wear this charm. Never let it out of your possession, and you will have nothing to fear during your voyage. Truly, you will be most favored."

He looked sharply at Musa again, took the money, glanced at it, and dropped it into a pouch.

"Do you really believe in the powers of your ornaments, then?" Musa asked skeptically.

Banasel's eyes widened, and he spread his arms. "To be sure," he said in a devout tone. "How can I believe else, when I have seen their miraculous workings so often?" He held up a hand. "Why, I could spend hours telling you of the powers these little ornaments possess, and of the miracles they have been responsible for. None have ever come to harm while wearing one of these enchanted talismans. None!" He spread his arms again.

Musa looked at him curiously. "I should like to hear your stories some day," he said politely.

He felt uncomfortable, as many people do when confronted by a confessed fanatic. His feelings were divided between surprise, a mild contempt, and an unease, born of wonder and uncertainty.

Obviously, the man was not especially favored. He was dressed like any street peddler. He had the slightly furtive, slightly brazen air of those who must avoid the anger, and sometimes the notice, of more powerful people, and yet, who must ply their trade. But he talked grandly of the immense powers of the baubles he vended, seeming to hold them in a sort of reverence. And, when he had spread his arms, there had been a short-lived hint of suppressed power. Musa shuddered a little.

"But I must go to the temple now, if I am to make arrangements for my voyage," he added apologetically. He turned away, then hurried down the street.

Banasel watched him go, a slight smile growing on his face.

"I don't blame you, Pal," he chuckled softly. "I'd feel the same way myself."

He glanced around noting a narrow alley. Casually, he walked into it, then looked around carefully. No one could observe him. He straightened, dropping the slightly disreputable, hangdog manner, then reached for his body shield controls.

Quickly, he cut out visibility, then actuated the levitator modulation and narrowed out of the alley, rose over the city, and headed toward the rugged mountains that formed the backbone of the island.

*****

Lanko was waiting, and quickly lowered the base shield.

"Well," he asked, "how did it go?"

"I found him." Banasel walked over to the cabinets, and started sorting the goods he had been carrying. "Sold him a miniature communicator. Now, I hope he wears the thing."

"We'll have to keep a close watch on him," commented Lanko, "just in case he puts it in his luggage and forgets about it. Did you give him a good sales talk?"

"Sure. Told him to wear it always. I pawed the air, raved a little, and made him think I was crazy. But I've an idea he'll remember and grab the thing if he sees trouble coming." Banasel put the last ornament in its place, and started unhooking his personal equipment. Then, he turned.

"Look," he commented, "why bother with all this mystic business? We've got mentacoms. Why not just clamp onto him, and keep track of him that way? It'd be a lot simpler. Less chance of a slip, too."

"Yeah, sure it would." Lanko gave his companion a disgusted look. "But have you ever tried that little trick?"

"No. I never had the occasion, but I've seen guardsmen run remote surveillances, and even exert control when necessary. They didn't have any trouble. We could try it, anyway."

Lanko sat up. "We could try it," he admitted, "but I know what would happen. I did try it once, and I found out a lot of things — quick." He looked into space for a moment. "How old are you, Banasel?"

"Why, you know that. I'm forty-one."

Lanko nodded. "So am I," he said. "And our civilization is a few thousand years old. And our species is somewhat older than that. We were in basic Guard training, and later in specialist philosophical training together. It took ten years, remember?"

"Sure. I remember every minute of it."

"Of course you do. It was that kind of training. But how old do you think some of those young guardsmen we worked with were?"

"Why, most of 'em were kids, fresh from school."

"That they were. But how many years — our years — had they spent in their schooling? How old were the civilizations they came from? And how old were their species?"

Lanko eyed him wryly.

Banasel looked thoughtfully across the room. "I never thought of it that way. Why, I suppose some of their forefathers were worrying about space travel before this planet was able to support life. And, come to think of it, I remember one of them making a casual remark about 'just a period ago,' when he was starting citizen training."

"That's what I mean." Lanko nodded emphatically. "'Just a period.' Only ten or twelve normal lifetimes for our kind of people. And his civilization's just as old compared to ours as he is compared to us — older, even.

"During that period he was so casual about, he was learning — practicing with his mind, so that the older citizens of the galaxy could make full contact with him without fear of injuring his mentality. He was learning concepts that he wouldn't dare even suggest to you or to me. Finally, after a few more periods, he'll begin to become mature. Do you think we could pick up all the knowledge and training back of his handling of technical equipment in a mere ten years of training?"

Banasel reached up, taking the small circlet from his head. He held it in his hand, looking at it with increased respect.

"You know," he admitted, "I really hadn't thought of it that way. They taught me to repair these things, among other pieces of equipment, and most of the construction is actually simple. They taught me a few uses for it, and I thought I understood it.

"Of course, I knew we were in contact with an advanced culture, and I knew that most of those guys we treated so casually had something that took a long time in the getting, but I didn't stop to think of the real stretch of time and study involved." He leaned back, replacing the mentacom on his head. "Somehow, they didn't make it apparent."

"Of course they didn't." Lanko spread his hands a little. "One doesn't deliberately give children a feeling of inferiority."

"Yeah. Will we ever learn?"

"Some. Some day. But we've got a long, lonely road to travel first." Lanko stood up and adjusted the communicator.

"Right now, though, we'd better keep tabs on Musa. In fact, we'd better follow him when he leaves here."

*****

The temple of Kondaro, the sea god, had been built at the edge of a cliff, so that it overlooked the Eastern Sea. The huge, white dome furnished a landmark for mariners far out at sea, and dominated the waterfront of Norlar. Atop the dome, a torch provided a beacon to relieve the blackness of moonless nights. This was the home of the crimson priests, and the center of guidance for all who wished to sail eastward.

27

Musa stood for some time, admiring the temple, then walked between the carefully clipped hedges and up the long line of steps leading to the arched entrance.

Again, he stopped. Overhead, the curved ceiling of the main dome was lower than its outer dimensions would lead one to believe, but Musa hardly noticed that. He gazed about the main rotunda.

It was predominantly blue. The dome was a smooth, blue sky, and the smooth blueness continued down the walls. The white stone steps were terminated at the edges of a mosaic sea, which stretched to the far walls, broken only by a large statue of the sea god. Kondaro stood in the center of his temple, facing the entrance. One arm stretched out, the hand holding a torch, while the other arm cradled one of the great ships favored by the god. Beneath one foot was one of the batlike sea demons, its face mirroring ultimate despair. About the feet lapped conventionally sculptured waves, which melted into the mosaic, to be continued to the walls by the pattern of the tiles. At the far side of the rotunda, the double stairs, which led to bronze doors, were almost inconspicuous, seeming to be a vaguely appearing mirage on the horizon of a limitless sea.

The trader looked at the far side, then down, and hesitated, feeling as though he were about to walk on water. Then, he turned, remembering the pedestal nearby. A crimson bowl rested on this stand, and beside it was a slave in the crimson loincloth which marked the menials of Kondaro.

Musa stepped over to the pedestal, dropped a coin into the bowl, and walked toward the rear of the temple, making proper obeisance to the huge statue. A young priest approached him.

"I crave blessings for a voyage I propose to take," announced the trader.

The priest inclined his head.

"Very well, Traveler, follow me."

He led the way to a small office. An older priest sat at a

28

large table, reading a tablet. Conveniently placed were writing materials, and on the table before him was another votive bowl. Musa dropped a coin into the bowl, and the priest looked up.

"I bring a voyager, O, Wise One," said the young priest.

"It is well," the older priest acknowledged in a deep voice. He turned to Musa. "Your name, Voyager?"

Musa gave his name, his age, the amount of his goods, and an account of his actions since his arrival in Tanagor. At the mention of Tonda, the priest nodded.

"The actions of Tonda have been most exemplary for the past several seasons," he remarked. "He is a good man, but he lacks the proper spirit of sacrifice." He concluded his writing.

"Well, then, Musa, you may go to those who sail ships with the blessing of Kondaro upon you. I shall only caution you as to the observance of the rites and laws for those who sail the Great Sea. Go now, in peace."

As Musa turned, the younger priest spoke. "I will lead you to one who will give you further guidance," he said.

Musa followed him to another small room, where he met still another priest. This man, he discovered, was a shrewd trader in his own right. He was familiar with goods and their values, and in addition to the rites he described, he presented definite advice as to what to take and what to leave behind. Fortunately, Musa discovered as he talked to this priest, he had picked very nearly as good a selection as he could wish.

During the days that followed, Musa made more votive offerings, practiced the rites ordered by the priest, and watched his goods as they were delivered to the *Bordeklu*, a ship belonging to Maladro, beloved of Kondaro, a shipowner whose ships were permitted by the sea god and his priests to sail the Eastern Sea.

At last, the day arrived when Musa himself boarded the ship and set sail past the headland of Norlar.

*****

As the ship was warped out of the harbor, Musa took stock of his fellow passengers. Among them were a slender, handsome man named Ladro, who had been on many previous voyages to the land of the East, and Min-ta, a native of the eastern continent, who was returning from a trading voyage to Norlar. There were several others, but they kept to themselves, seeming to radiate an aura of exclusiveness. Ladro and Min-ta on the other hand, were more approachable.

Surely, thought Musa, these two can teach me a great deal of the land I am to visit, if they will.

He walked over to the rail, where the two stood, looking out over the shoreline. The ship was coming abreast of the great temple of Kondaro.

"It's the most prominent landmark on the island, isn't it?" Musa commented.

"What?" Ladro turned, looking at him curiously. "Oh, yes," he said, "the temple. Yes, it's the last thing you see as

30

you leave, and the first when you return." He paused, examining Musa. "This is your first trip?"

"Yes, it is. I've always traded ashore before this."

"But you finally decided to visit Kneuros?"

"Yes. I've dealt with a few traders who had goods from there, and their stories interested me."

Ladro smiled. "Romance of the far places?"

"Well, there's that, too," Musa admitted, "but I'm interested in some of the merchandise I've seen."

"There's profit in it," agreed Ladro. "How long have you been trading around Norlar?"

"This is my first trip. I'm from Karth, in the Galankar."

"You mean you were never in Norlar before?" Min-ta joined the conversation.

Musa shook his head. "I left Karth for the purpose of trading east of the Great Sea."

"Unusual," mused Min-ta. "Most traders work between Tanagor and the mainland for several years before they try the Sea."

"Yes," added Ladro, "and some never go out. They satisfy themselves with the channel trade." He pointed. "We're getting out to the open sea now, past the reef."

The ship drew away from the island kingdom, setting its course toward the vague horizon. The day wore on, to be replaced by the extreme blackness of night. Then, the sky lit up again, heralding another day.

The ship's company had settled to sea routine, and the traders roamed about their portion of the deck, talking sometimes, or napping in the sun. Musa leaned over the low rail, watching the water, and admiring the clear, blue swells.

He raised his head as the door of the forward cabins opened. A priest, followed by a group of slaves, went up to the raised forecastle. Under the priest's direction, the slaves busied themselves putting up a high, crimson and yellow curtain across the foredeck. They completed their task and went below.

31

Again, the door opened, and a procession, headed by the chief priest, slowly mounted the ladder to the forecastle. Each of the three priests was followed by his slave, who bore a crimson casket. The curtain closed behind them, then the slaves came out and ranged themselves across the deck, facing aft.

"I wonder," said Musa, turning to Ladro, "what ritual they are performing."

Ladro shook his head. "The less a man knows of the activities of the priests, the better he fares," he declared. "Truly, on a great ship, curiosity is a deadly vice."

Musa nodded to the stern. "I see that one of the priests is not at the bow."

"That is right. One priest always remains by the steersman, to ward off the spells of the sea demons." Ladro paused, pointing overside. "See," he said in a pleased tone, "here is an envoy from Kondaro."

*****

Musa's gaze followed the pointing finger. A huge fish was cruising alongside, gliding effortlessly through the waves, and occasionally leaping into the air.

"An envoy?"

"Yes. So long as a kontar follows a ship, fair weather and smooth sailing may be expected. They are sent by Kondaro as guardians for those ships he especially favors."

At a call from the priest in the stern, two sailors appeared, carrying chunks of meat. As the priest chanted, they tossed these overside. The great fish rose from the water, catching one of the chunks as it fell, then dropped back, and the water frothed whitely as he retrieved the other. He gulped the meat, then swam contentedly, still pacing the ship.

"Suppose someone fell overboard?" Musa gazed at the kontar in fascination.

Ladro and Min-ta exchanged glances.

"If one is favored by the Great One," replied Min-ta slowly, "it is believed that the kontar would guard him

32

from harm. Otherwise, the sacrifice would be accepted."

Musa looked at the clear water, then glanced back to the spot of foam which drew astern.

"I don't believe I'll try any swimming from the ship." He backed slightly from the rail, glancing quickly at Ladro and Min-ta, then looking away again.

He suddenly realized that he had exceeded his quota of questions, and that he could get into trouble. He had noted that most of the ship's company appeared to know the other traders aboard, even though some of them hadn't been to sea before. Min-ta and Ladro were obviously well acquainted with several of the ship's officers. But he, Musa, was a stranger.

He had already observed that the priesthood of Kondaro was not averse to a quick profit, and that they placed a low value on the lives and possessions of others. He had dealt with tribes ashore, who had the simple, savage ethic:

"He is a stranger? Kill him! Take his goods, and kill him."

Ashore, he had protected himself during his many trips by consorting with other traders of good reputation, and by hiring guards. But here? He remembered the remarks made by Kerunar back in Manotro.

"When I face the thief or the bandit, I prefer to have a weapon in my hand."

Slowly, he collected himself, and looked back at Ladro and Min-ta.

"If you gentlemen will excuse me," he apologized, "I have some accounts to cast, so I believe I'll go to my quarters." He turned and went below.

As he disappeared down the ladder, Ladro turned to his companion.

"Of course," he said thoughtfully, "if all goes well, this man will be most favored. But if the Great One shows signs of displeasure — "

Min-ta nodded. "Yes," he agreed, "I have heard of strangers who excited the wrath of Kondaro." His eyes

33

narrowed speculatively. "Those of the faithful who keep watch on such unfavored beings are rewarded by the priests, I am told."

Ladro nodded. "I believe that is correct," he agreed. "We should be watchful for impiety in any event." He stretched. "Well, I think I shall take a short nap before dinner."

Below, the traders' quarters were cramped. There was a small, common space, with a table, over which hung the single light. About the bulkheads were curtained recesses, sufficiently large for a bunk and with barely enough space for the occupant to stand. Musa closed the curtains, and sat down on his bunk.

Of course, he had no proof. There was no really logical sequence to prove that the situation was dangerous. There was no evidence that his fellow voyagers were other than honorable, well-intentioned men. But he simply didn't feel right. He pulled his wooden chest from under the bunk, opened it, and looked through the small store of personal effects.

There was no weapon. The law of Kondaro forbade the carrying of those by other than the priests and their slaves. His attention was attracted by a glitter, and he picked up the small amulet he had bought from the peddler in Norlar. Slowly, he turned it in his hands.

It was an unusual ornament, strangely wrought. He had never seen such fine, regular detail, even in the best handicraft. As he looked closer, he could not see how it could have been accomplished with any of the instruments he was familiar with, yet it must have been hand made, unless it were actually of supernatural origin.

He remembered the urgent seriousness of the peddler's attitude, and he could recall some of his words. The man had spoken almost convincingly of powerful protectors, and Musa could foresee the need of such. He found himself speaking.

"Oh, power that rests in this amulet," he said, "if there

34

is any truth in the peddler's words, I — " He paused, his usual, hard, common sense taking over.

"I'm being silly!" He drew his hand back to throw the ornament into the chest. Then, he felt himself stopped. An irresistible compulsion seized him, and he dazedly secured the amulet about his neck. Feeling sick and weak, he tucked it into his garments. Then, still moving in a daze, he left the cabin and returned to the deck. He did not so much as try to resist the sudden desire.

The breeze made him feel a little better, but he was still shaken, and his head ached violently. Little snatches of undefined memory tried to creep into his consciousness, but he couldn't quite bring them into focus. He turned toward the rail, and saw Min-ta still there.

"Well," commented the easterner, "your accounts didn't take long."

Musa smiled wanly. "It was stuffy down there. I felt I had to come up for some air."

Min-ta nodded. "It does get close in the quarters during the day." He pointed alongside.

"We are favored still," he said. "Another kontar has joined us."

Two of the great fish paced the ship, gliding and leaping effortlessly from wave to wave. Musa watched them.

"We must be favored indeed."

"Yes." Min-ta smiled. "May our favor last."

Musa's head still ached, and the glints of the sun reflected from the water made it worse. He looked aft, to the faint line where sky met water. There was a low line of clouds. His gaze traveled along the horizon, and he noted that the clouds seemed a little darker forward. Still, he felt uneasy, and alone.

*****

"See what I meant?"

"Ooh! Yeah. Yeah, I see. What a backlash that was! I've got the grandfather of all headaches, and I won't be able to think straight for a week. Wonder how Musa feels — But I got results, anyway."

"Yes. You got results. So did I once, when I tried something similar. But I'll live a long time before I try it again. How about you?"

"Don't worry. Next time I try to exert direct mental control on another entity, this planet'll have space travel. Wonder if some klordon tablets'll help any."

"Might. Try one, then let's get busy and scatter a few more communicators around that ship. Be more practical than beating our brains out."

*****

As the days passed, Musa became familiar with the shipboard routine and lost some of his early uneasiness regarding his traveling companions. He became acquainted with other traders, finding them to be average men, engaged in the same trade as himself. He talked to members of the ship's company, and found them to be normal men, who worked at their trade in a competent manner. Only the four priests held aloof. Ignoring officers, sailors, and traders alike, they spoke only to their slaves, who passed their comments to the ship's company.

On the morning of the tenth day, Musa came to the deck, to find the sea rougher than usual. Waves rose, scattering their white plumes for the wind to scatter. Ahead, dark clouds hid the sky, and occasional spray came aboard, spattering the deck and the passengers.

Just outside the cabin entrance, a small knot of traders were gathered. As Musa came out, they separated.

Musa went over to the rail, looking overside at the waves. The two kontars were not in sight. He looked about, noting the sailors, who hurried about the deck and into the rigging, securing their ship for foul weather. Close by, Ladro and Min-ta were talking.

"It is quite possible," said Ladro, "that someone aboard has broken a law of the great Kondaro, and the kontars have gone to report the sin." He glanced at Musa

36

calculatingly.

"Yes," agreed Min-ta, "we — "

An officer, hurrying along the deck, stopped. "All passengers will have to go below," he said. "We're in for bad weather, and don't want to lose anyone overboard."

"Could this be the wrath of Kondaro?" asked Ladro.

The officer glanced at him questioningly. "It could be, yes. Why?"

Again, Ladro cast a look at Musa, then he caught the seaman by the arm, pulling him aside. The two engaged in a low-toned conversation, directing quick glances at Musa. At last, the officer nodded and went aft, to approach one of the slaves of Kondaro.

Musa started across the deck to the ladder, his heart thudding painfully. Surely, he thought, he had done nothing to offend even the most particular of deities. Yet, the implications of Ladro's glances and his conversation with the ship's officer were too obvious for even the dullest to misinterpret. Musa took a long, shuddering breath.

His fears on that other day had been well grounded, then.

He gazed at the lowering sky, then out at the waves. Where could a lone, friendless man find help in this waste of wind and water?

Slowly, he climbed down the ladder leading to his tiny cubicle.

Once inside, he again started checking over his personal items. There was nothing there to help. Hopelessly, he looked at the collection in the chest, then he got out a scroll of prose and went to the central table to read in an effort to clear his mind of the immediate circumstances.

Minutes later, he went back to his bunk and threw the scroll aside. Possibly, he was just imagining that he was the target of a plot. Possibly there was a real sea god named Kondaro — an omnipotent sea deity, who could tell when persons within his domain were too curious, or harbored impious thoughts, and who was capable of influencing the actions of the faithful.

Possibly, his opinions of the priesthood had been noted and had offended. Or, perhaps, that peculiar little device he had seen a priest studying was capable of warning the god that it had been profaned by an unsanctified gaze. Possibly, this storm was really the result of such a warning. He was sure the priest hadn't seen him, but it could be that the device itself might —

Musa threw himself on his bunk.

*****

A deep voice resonated through the room.

"Musa of Karth," it said, "my master, Dontor, desires your presence on deck."

Musa came to his feet. Two of the slaves of Kondaro stood close by, swords in hand. One beckoned, then turned. Musa followed him into the short passage, and up the ladder. As they gained the deck, the small procession turned aft, to face the senior priest.

Dontor stood on the raised after deck, just in front of the helmsman. The wind tugged at his gold and crimson robe, carrying it away from his body, so that it rippled like a flag, and exposed the bright blue trousers and jacket. Dontor, chief priest of the *Bordeklu*, stood immobile, his arms folded, his feet braced against the sway of his vessel. As the trio below him stopped, he frowned down at them.

"Musa, of Karth," he intoned, "it has been revealed to me that you have displayed undue curiosity as to the inner mysteries of the worship of the Great God. In your conversations, you have hinted at knowledge forbidden any but the initiated.

"You came to us, a stranger, and we trusted you. But now, we are all faced with the wrath of the Great One as a result of your impieties. A sacrifice, and only a sacrifice, will appease this wrath. Can you name any reason why we should protect you further, at the expense of our own lives? What say you?"

Musa stared up at him. The cotton in his throat had

38

suddenly become thick, and intensely bitter. Unsuccessfully, he tried to swallow, and a mental flash told him that whatever he said, he was already convicted. Regardless of what defense he might offer, he knew he would be condemned to whatever punishment these people decided to deal out to him. And that punishment, he realized, would be death. He straightened proudly.

"Oh, priest," he said thickly, "I am guilty of no crime. You, however, are about to commit a serious crime, which is beyond my power to prevent." He hesitated, then continued. "Be warned, however, that if there are any real gods above or below, you will receive punishment. The gods, unlike men, are just!"

Aware of sudden motion in his direction, he rapidly finished.

"So, make your sacrifice, and then see if you can save your vessel from the natural forces of wind and water."

The priest stiffened angrily.

"Blasphemy," he said. "Blasphemy, of the worst sort." He looked away from Musa. "I believe that in this case, the Great One will require the ship's company to deal with you in their own way, that they may be purged of any contamination due to your presence." He raised his arms.

"Oh, Great Kondaro, Lord of all the seas, and the things within the seas," he began.

Musa evaded the two slaves with a quick weave of his shoulders. Covering the distance to the side of the ship with a few quick steps, he jumped over the rail. As he fell, the wind tore at him, and his windmilling arms and legs failed to find any purchase to right him.

He hit the water with a splash and concussion that nearly knocked the breath from his body, and promptly sank. As the water closed over his head, he struck out with hands and feet in an effort to climb again to light and air. His head broke the surface, and he flailed the water in an effort to keep his nose in air. The ship was drawing away from him, its storm sails set.

As he struggled in the water, he wondered if it was worth while. After all, he had only to allow himself to sink, and all his troubles would be over shortly. Wouldn't it be easier to do this than to continue torturing himself with a hopeless fight?

Too, he wondered if he had been right in leaving the ship, but he quickly dismissed that thought. The sea was impersonal, neither cruel nor kind. It was far better, he thought, to surrender to the forces of nature than to subject himself to the viciousness of angry men.

Suddenly, a constraining force seized him. He instinctively fought to free himself, then realized that he was being drawn upward, out of the water. Possibly, he thought, the Great One wanted to speak to him.

*****

He rose swiftly through the air, passed through complete darkness for an instant, then found himself in a small room. Two men stood facing him, both of them vaguely familiar. As his mind refocused, Musa recognized the peddler of amulets, then the herder to whom he had once sold a sword. They were strangely familiar, but they were in strange costumes. He stared at them.

"Well, Musa," said the herder. "I see you got into trouble."

Musa blinked. "Who are you?" he demanded. "How do you know of my affairs?"

The peddler of amulets grinned. "Why, we are old companions, Musa," he said. "Of course, you have forgotten us, but we never forgot you." He pointed.

"This is Resident Guardsman Lanko. I am Banasel, also of the Stellar Guard. Our job is to prevent just such situations as the one you just found yourself in." His grin faded. "That, and a few other things."

Musa frowned. "Stellar Guard? What is that?"

Lanko studied him for a moment, then crossed the small room. "You knew once," he tossed over his shoulder, "but you rejected the knowledge, and it had to be taken from you. Since you'll be working with us for a while, I think we will have to restore your memories. Perhaps you'll want to retain them." He removed equipment from a cabinet.

"Some of this will have to be secondhand, since neither Banasel nor myself have been in the spots shown. But some of it is firsthand."

His hand flicked a switch.

A power unit hummed, and Musa found himself recalling a campsite near the now destroyed and rebuilt city of Atakar. As the imposed mental blocks fell away, he remembered who Banasel and Lanko were. And he realized why he had been drawn to them in the recent past.

Memories of his days of slavery in Atakar flashed before his mind, and he remembered the part these two had taken in his escape. He recalled the days of banditry, and the strange visitors, who had brought with them disturbing knowledge, and strange powers.

He saw the destruction of Atakar, and the capture of the galactic criminals who had depraved that city. He shared the experiences of his two companions during their introduction to the advanced culture of the Galactic Federation, and he saw snatches of their training at Aldebaran Base. He went with them on some of their missions.

The humming stopped, and he looked up at the two.

"So," Lanko told him, "now you know."

Musa nodded. "I turned something down, didn't I?"

*****

As Musa disappeared over the vessel's side, the priest, Dontor, lowered his arms. Quickly turning the unscheduled event to advantage, he cried, "We need worry no further, my children. The Great One has called this blasphemer to final account."

He turned to one of his juniors, lowering his voice.

"Go below, Alnar, and break out this man's goods. We must reward those who informed us."

The junior bowed. "Yes, sir." He hesitated. "Will this

storm blow over soon?" he queried.

Dontor smiled. "You should have paid more attention to your course in practical seamanship," he chided. "We are sailing fairly close hauled, so our speed is added to that of the wind. And, since storms move, it'll pass us shortly." He pointed to the horizon.

"See that small break in the clouds? That indicates a possibility of clear weather beyond. We should be through the worst of the storm in a matter of a few hours. And we'll never reach the really dangerous core of the storm, for we are passing through an edge of it. Our only problem is to keep from losing a mast during the time we are close to the storm's heart." He paused, looking aloft.

"The crew is competent. They have the sails properly reefed, and, if necessary, they can furl them in short order. What trouble can we have?"

"Thank you, sir." The younger priest bowed again. "I will make the necessary arrangements for those goods."

Dontor stood for a moment, surveying the ship, then walked toward the helm.

"If I am ever in charge of operations," he told himself, "I will replace some of these sailors by neophyte priests, and let them steer by their own compasses. This method is too cumbersome. Besides, the neophytes should get to sea earlier, anyway."

He approached the pilot priest, who stood apart from the helmsman, his slave holding the little red box with the compass.

"How is our course?"

The priest turned, then bowed. "We are off course twelve degrees to the north, sir," he reported. "I have instructed the helmsman to come as close to the wind as possible."

Dontor nodded. "Very good," he approved. "Keep track of your time, and we'll correct when we get a chance to shift course to the south. We can determine whatever final correction is necessary at noon sight tomorrow."

Alnar came up the ladder to the quarterdeck. Approaching Dontor, he bowed in salute, then reported.

"The goods are ready, sir."

"Very well. Find those two traders and give them the usual ten per cent, then bring me an inventory of the remainder."

*****

Musa stood, fists clenched, facing the recorder play-back. "The usual ten per cent, he says! Why, I'd like to slaughter the lot of those murdering thieves!"

Lanko snapped off the switch. "Don't blame them too much," he laughed. "After all, they're only trying to make a living, and it's the only trade they know."

As Musa nearly choked on his attempted reply, Banasel broke in.

"Sure," he chuckled. "Besides, it's guys like them that keep guys like us in business."

Lanko noticed the horrified expression on Musa's face, and quickly composed himself. He put his hand on the man's shoulder.

"Look," he explained seriously, "if we got so we took people like these to heart, we'd spend half our time getting psyched to unsnarl our own mental processes." He gestured to the reels of tape in a cabinet.

"Here, we have the records of hundreds of cases like this one. Some are worse, some are not so bad. Every one of them had to be — and was — cracked by members of our Corps. This is just another of those minor, routine incidents that keep cropping up all over the galaxy. It's our problem now, and we'll get to work on it." He turned.

"Where do you want to start, Banasel?"

"Well — competition's the life of trade."

"That comes later." Lanko shook his head. "There's an alien or so to be taken care of first, you know."

"I know. It's fairly obvious."

43

"So, we've got to find him — or them."

Musa had regained his self-control. "What about these birds in hand?"

Banasel shrugged. "Small fry. We'll take care of them later." He walked over to the workbench, picking up Lanko's sword.

"I wondered about this before," he said. "Now, I'm sure about it. It simply doesn't match a normal technology for this period."

Musa looked at him curiously. "But there are a lot of those around Norlar," he said. "They're a rarity in the Galankar, to be sure, but — "

"That's what we mean," Lanko told him. "Too many anachronisms. First, we have this sword. Then, we meet these priests of Kondaro, who discuss meteorology, navigation, and pilotage with considerable understanding. We've had communicators planted on that ship for several days now, and I still can't see how the technology was developed that allowed the manufacture of some of their instruments. We should have noticed something wrong a long time ago.

"The priests use sextants, watches, compasses. And, just to make it worse, we have one video recording of a priest laying out a course on an accurate chart. He was using a protractor, which was divided into Galactic degrees. That was the clincher. Somebody's out of place, and we've got to find him — or them."

He took the sword from Banasel. "I think we'd better go on to the eastern continent, see what we can find, then we can deal with our friends. But first, Ban, you'd better run out a call for one of the Sector Guardsmen to back us up if necessary. We could run into something too hot for us to handle."

Banasel nodded and turned to the communicator. Lanko dropped into the pilot seat, glanced at the screens, and moved controls. In the viewscreen, the sea tilted, drew farther away, then became a level, featureless blue expanse.

"Well, here's your eastern continent. In fact, this is the city of Kneuros. It's where you wanted to go, isn't it?"

Musa looked at Banasel thoughtfully.

"Yes," he admitted. "It's where I thought I wanted to go, but now I really know what I wanted in the first place."

"Oh?"

"Certainly. I was restless. I thought I liked being a trader in Karth, and I was a fairly good trader, too. But I was just getting things at secondhand. I turned down just what I really wanted, because it scared me. That was a long time ago." He looked at the control panel. He'd understood such panels once, some years ago.

"How do you plan to find your aliens — if there are any?"

"Search pattern." Lanko shrugged. "We'll cruise around in a grid pattern until we pick up some sort of reading, or until we spot something abnormal." He pointed at a series of instruments.

"They're bound to have a ship somewhere, and we'll pick up a small amount of power radiation from their screens. If their ship were orbiting in space, we'd have picked it up long ago, so we must assume it's grounded. I think we'd better go right into a pattern. We can use Kneuros as origin." He stared at the plotting instruments.

"Let's see. If I wanted to hide a ship, I'd use the most inaccessible location I could find. We do that ourselves, in fact. And there are some mountainous regions inland." He set up course and speed.

"Yeah," Banasel added, "and I'd worry a lot more about ground approach than air accessibility, at least on this planet."

The ship gained altitude, accelerated, and sped eastward.

Day by day, the course trace built up, the cameras recorded the terrain under the ship, and the two guardsmen built up their mosaic. The ship crossed and re-crossed the continent, mapping as it went.

From time to time, Lanko made careful comparison of the new mosaic with an earlier survey, noting differences. There were new settlements. Where members of a nomadic culture had roamed the prairie, an industrial civilization was rapidly growing.

Lanko tapped on the map. "Two cultures," he observed. "Two cultures, separated by mountains and desert. Absolutely no evidence of contact, but considerable similarity between them. This pattern begins to look familiar."

He picked a tape from the shelves, ran it through a viewer, then reversed it, and picked out various portions for recheck. Finally, he made a superposition of some of their observation tape, examined it, and turned. Banasel held up a hand.

"Don't tell us," he growled. "I studied about drones, too."

"Drones?" Musa looked at him, then glanced back at the viewer.

"Yes. Characters from one of the advanced cultures, who feel frustrated, and fail to fit in. They often turn into pleasure seekers, and frequently end up by monkeying with primitive cultures, to prove their ability to themselves, at least."

"Things like this happen often?"

"Oh, not too often, I suppose, but often enough so that people like us are stationed on every known primitive planet, to prevent activity of the type. You see, the drones usually start out simply, by setting up minor interference in business or government on some primitive planet. Usually, they're caught pretty quickly. But sometimes they evade capture. And they can end up by exerting serious influence in cultural patterns. Some planets have been set back, and even destroyed as a result of drone activity. Although their motives are different, drones're just as bad and just as dangerous as any other criminal."

Lanko grinned a little. "Only difference is, they're usually easier to combat than organized criminal groups with a real purpose. Generally, they're irresponsible youngsters who don't have the weapons, organization, or ability that the real criminals come up with." He shrugged.

"Of course," he added, "we've called for help just in case. But we'll probably be able to take care of this situation by ourselves. In fact, unless there are unusual features, we'd better, if we don't want to be regarded as somewhat ineffectual." He paused, glanced toward the detector set, and tapped on the map again, then slowly traced out an area.

"We should be picking up something pretty soon," he said, thoughtfully. "Better set up a pattern around here, in the mountain ranges, Banasel. We can worry about settled areas later."

*****

A needle flickered, rose from zero, then steadied.

Somewhere, back of the instrument panel, a tiny current actuated a micro relay, and an alarm drop fell.

As the warning buzz sounded, both Lanko and Banasel looked over at the detector panel.

"Well, it's about time." Lanko leaned to his right, setting switches. A screen lit up, showing a faint, red dot. He touched the controls, bringing the dot to center screen, then checked the meters.

"Not too far," he remarked. "A little out of normal range, though. He must have all his screen power on."

Banasel turned back to the workbench, studied the labels on the drawers for a moment, then opened one.

"Guess we'll need a can opener?"

"We might. If he's aboard, we may have to get a little rough." Lanko leaned back.

"Check the power pattern. Sort of like to know what we're running into before we commit ourselves." He glanced again at the indicators, then poked at switches.

"In fact, I think we'd better wait right here, till we get

this boy identified."

Banasel was whistling tunelessly as he set up readings on a computer. Finally, he poked the activator bar, and watched as the machine spat out tape. Above the tape chute, a series of graphs indicated the computations, but Banasel ignored them, feeding the tape into another machine.

"I suppose there are some characters who could make a positive identification from the figures and curves. But I'm just a beginner. That's why they furnish integrator directories, I guess."

Lanko smiled. "I don't know anything, either," he agreed. "But I generally know where I can look up what I need." He set a compact reel of tape into the computer.

They watched the directory as its screens glowed. Figures and descriptions shimmered, and there was a rapid ticking. A sheet flowed out toward them, and Banasel tore it off as the ticks ceased.

"Type seventeen screens," he read. "Probably Ietorian model Nan fifty-seven generators. Strictly a sportster setup. He's got electromagnetics and physical contact screens, but there's nothing else. And, with the type of readings I've got here, I'd say he's running all the power he's got. Do we go in?"

"Sure we do." Lanko nodded confidently as he slapped the drive lever.

"This thing we've got's only an atmosphere flier, but it's made to take care of tougher stuff than luxury sportsters. Set up your can opener, just in case our boy wants to argue with us."

Banasel nodded silently.

The small sportster was parked between two peaks. Before it was a tiny level space, too small for any ship. Above it, towered bare rock, tipped with eternal snow. Lanko examined the scene disgustedly.

"Inhospitable, isn't he?" he grunted. "He could at least have had enough front yard for a visitor to land." He picked up a microphone, touched a stud, and turned a knob. A faint hiss sounded from the speaker before him.

"Philcor resident calling sportster," he snapped. "Come in, Over."

The hiss continued. Lanko punched another stud, and listened. The hiss remained unchanged.

"Open him up, Banasel," he finally ordered. "I'm going in."

He rose from his chair, crossing to the exit port. For an instant, he stood, checking his equipment belt. Then, he reached to a cabinet, to pick up a tool kit. He opened the box, examined its contents, then turned and nodded to Banasel.

The port opened wide, and he stepped through.

He dropped lightly to the space before the sportster, then stepped away, crouching behind a rock out-crop, and turned his body shield to full power.

"Screens down," he ordered.

*****

A faint haze grew about the sportster. At first, it was a barely perceptible fluorescence. Then, it became a fiercely incandescent glow. It flamed for a few seconds, then faded, becoming green, yellow, red, and at last, blinking to invisibility.

"They're damped," Banasel's voice announced. "Shall I give him some more and knock out the generators?"

"Not necessary," Lanko told him. "Just hold complete neutralization. I'll cut them from inside."

He rose from his position behind the rock, idly kicking at the face of it as he walked past. A shower of dust crumbled to the ground.

"Good thing there aren't any trees around here," he laughed. "We'd have to put out a forest fire."

He pulled his hand weapon from his belt, made a careful adjustment, then walked over to the ship. After a quick examination, he directed the weapon toward a spot in the hull.

"Lot of credits here," he commented laconically. "Shame to hurt the finish too much."

A few minutes later, he stepped back, examining his work. Then, he nodded and removed another instrument from his tool kit. He focused it on the ship's port, flicked a switch on his belt, then snapped the instrument on.

For a few seconds, nothing happened, then there was a grinding screech of tortured metal, and the port swung open.

As Lanko stepped inside, he examined the control room with care. At last, satisfied that no booby traps were set, he crossed to the control panel. He located the communicator controls, and picked up the microphone.

"All's well, Ban," he reported. "Ease off."

He watched as the overloaded generator recovered. When the needles were at normal readings, he flicked the screen controls off, then picked up the microphone again.

"Haul out, Banasel," he ordered. "I'm going to fix this can up again, close the port, run up the screens, and wait for our boy to come home. Like to talk to him."

*****

The sportster had a well stocked galley. Lanko ate with enjoyment, studying the tapes he had found interestedly. Finally, he pushed the last reel aside, then sat back to gaze at the wall.

A low tone sounded, and the viewscreen activated. Lanko nodded to himself, then went to the control room aperture, turning off the alarm as he went through. A few strides took him to the entry port, where he waited, weapon in hand.

The door swung open and Lanko touched his trigger. The newcomer's screen flared briefly, then collapsed. Lanko stepped forward, examining his prisoner.

He was humanoid. There were some differences from the usual type encountered on the planet, but they were not serious. He could have passed in most of the Galankar, if not anywhere. Some might even be attracted by his slightly unusual appearance. Lanko drew him into the ship, and closed the port.

He took his time, making a complete search of the captive's clothing, and removing equipment and weapons. At last, he drew back, satisfied that the being was harmless. He waited. It wouldn't be too long before the business could begin.

As the paralysis effect wore off, the man on the floor flexed his muscles, then got to his feet. Lanko watched him, his weapon resting on his knees. As the man tensed to spring, Lanko raised the weapon a little.

"You are Genro Kir?"

"Who are you? What's the idea?" Kir reached for his belt, then dropped his hand again as he found nothing there.

"Resident Guardsman. Name's Lanko. You seem to be a little out of place on this planet."

"I'm not responsible to some native patrolman." Kir's face became stubborn. "I'm a Galactic Citizen."

"Possibly. We'll leave that to the Sector authorities." Lanko shrugged, his face expressionless. "Meantime, you'll have to accept things as they are. Or would you rather be paralyzed again?"

Genro Kir tensed again, making an obvious mental effort.

Lanko grinned at him in real amusement. "I took it. Wouldn't do you much good anyway. They gave me heavy-duty equipment, you know." He waved toward a chair with his weapon. "Might as well sit down and talk about it. I've been through your tapes, of course."

Kir looked around unhappily, then sank into a chair. "What's there to talk about, then? You know what we were doing."

"In general, yes, we do. A good deal was on your tapes. But we need more detail, and we've got to pick up your companions, you know. It would be a lot better if we knew where they were."

"I don't know where they are myself. They're building

51

up their forces, and working for position. This is just the opening, you see. The real game won't start for quite a while."

Lanko laughed shortly. "Frankly, I don't think it will start. But it would make it simpler for all concerned if you'd help us find the players."

"I told you. I don't know where they are. They don't have to tell the referee every move they make, unless they want a consultation as to legality. I was just keeping watch on the general picture, to see that neither of them broke a rule, or took an unfair advantage."

"You may not know where they are," Lanko admitted, "but you can certainly contact them."

Genro Kir smiled tightly. "But I won't."

"They'll be hunted down, you know. We'll have them eventually. Be a lot easier for all concerned if you'd coöperate."

"Coöperate with a bunch of half savage natives, against my own friends? Don't be more stupid than you have to be!"

"I see." Lanko glanced away. "All very ethical, of course. Well, in that case, we'll have to go to work." He pulled a fine chain from a case at his belt, and walked over to his captive, weapon ready.

"Just hold still," he ordered. He slipped the delicate looking necklace over the man's head, squeezed the pendant, and jumped back.

"I don't know whether you're familiar with this device," he said, "so I'll explain it to you. It's a type ninety-two gravitic manacle, and is designed to hold any known being. You can move about freely, so long as you don't make any sudden or violent motion. The device is keyed to my shield, and you'll suffer temporary paralysis if you get within my near zone. You're safe enough a couple of meters from me." He walked back to the control console.

"Oh, yes," he added, "don't try to take it off. It's designed to prevent that action by positive means. It won't do you any permanent damage, but it can make you pretty uncomfortable. And, remember, if it becomes necessary, I can activate the manacle. It'll put you into full paralysis and send out a strong homing signal."

Genro Kir looked at him sourly. "I won't try to escape," he promised.

"That's immaterial to me." Lanko flicked switches and the ship rose from the ground, swung, and started westward. "I was merely describing the capabilities of the manacle."

*****

On the way over the sea, Lanko noted the positions of a few of the trading ships, and approached them closely, examining them. As he approached a small archipelago, his communicator screen brightened.

"Resident Guardsman to Sportster. Identity yourself. Over."

Lanko picked up the microphone. "It's all right, Ban. Got one. Two more to go."

"Fair enough. Come on in. I've got a beam on you."

Lanko checked the approach scope. The small circle was a trifle out of center. He touched the control bar, and as the circle centered, he snapped a switch and sat back.

The sportster dipped over an island, crossed a narrow lagoon, and settled to the ground beside the guard flier. Lanko started pulling tools from his kit. Working carefully, he removed the cover from the control console, examined the terminal blocks, then attached a small cylinder between two terminals.

He closed the console again and walked over to the exit port, where he pressed the emergency release. The port swung wide. For an instant, the control console was blurred. Lanko waited, then as the panel returned to focus, he walked back to it. He snapped the drive switch on and pushed the drive to maximum. Nothing happened. He punched the emergency power button, and waited an instant. There was no result. He nodded to his prisoner.

"Come on, Genro Kir. We may want you to talk to someone." He pointed to the port. Kir hesitated, then went through. He managed a sneer as he did so.

The port of the flier opened, and Banasel looked out. "Need any help?"

"No. This spaceship won't fly till someone from Sector comes out to pull the block." Lanko pointed. "This is Genro Kir. He was refereeing a sort of battle game between a couple of his companions."

Lanko herded Kir in front of him, and entered his own flier. He placed the equipment kit on a shelf, and sat down. Banasel perched on his workbench.

"What kind of a setup did these jokers have?"

"Well, you can review the tapes later and get a few of the details, but here's the general idea:

"Genro Kir and his two companions made planetfall some years back. They didn't know it was a discovered planet, and failed to note any evidence of our presence. Somehow, we missed them, too, for which we should hang our heads.

"Anyway, they checked the planet, found it was suitable to their purpose, and decided that Koree Buron and Sira Nal could use it as a playing board. Seems they had a bet on, and their last game was inconclusive. Both of the involved civilizations collapsed.

"Each of them selected a portion of the habitable part of the eastern continent as a primary base. Buron took the east, and that left the west to Nal. It so happens that the central portion of the continent is difficult to pass, and that fitted in with their plans. You remember the desert and mountain ranges, of course? Well, so far as I can discover, there was virtually no contact before the arrival of these three prizes of ours. And after their arrival, they made sure that there would be no contact — not until they wanted it.

"Of course, deserts can be crossed, and mountains can be climbed, but our three boys fixed it so it would be fatal for any native to try it. Then, each of the two contestants set to work to build up the war potential of his part of the continent.

"In the meantime, Genro was acting as referee. He's been checking the progress of the two contestants, and making sure that neither of them sneaks into the territory of the other to upset something, or commits any other breach of rules."

Banasel slid off his bench. "Atmosphere of mutual trust, I see."

"Precisely."

"Where do the Kondaran priests come in?"

"Oh, those two aren't going to confine the final stage of their game to the one continent. That's just the starting point — the home base. And what they're doing now is just the opening of the game. The end game will decide control of the entire planet. Sira Nal's just getting off to an early start, that's all."

"This is legitimate, according to their rules?"

"I guess so. According to Kir's tapes, he thinks it's a clever maneuver. 'Sound move' is the way he expressed it." Lanko stood and walked over to the reproducer set. "That all came from the tapes, of course."

"How much more has Kir told you?"

"As little as possible."

*****

Banasel looked toward the prisoner. "Why not coöperate? You're due for Aldebaran anyway. And a little help now would make it easier for you and your partners later."

Genro Kir's lip curled. "As I told your friend, I don't have to lower myself to work with a bunch of low-grade primitives."

"See what I mean?" Lanko slanted an eyebrow at Banasel. "But I think our friend here will help us some, anyway. That 'sound move' he recorded is almost sure to catch us one of the players."

"Oh?"

55

"Sure. What's the whole foundation of this cult of Kondaro?"

"Why, they navigate ships. They keep strict security on their methods. They enforce that security by terrorism. They claim that no one else can successfully cross the Great Sea, and it seems to be a proven fact that they're right. So, they collect from seamen, traders, and shipowners."

"That's right. And they claim that only they can overcome the spells and actions of the sea demons, which try to destroy any ship that sails the sea. First, though, they navigate ships. They guarantee to get 'em across the sea and back. Right?"

Banasel nodded.

"Suppose they start losing ships? Suppose that from now on, no ship returns to port?" Lanko walked over to the control console.

"Hey, wait a minute. I know these priests are a bunch of pirates — or some of them are, at any rate. But we can't —"

"Who said anything about destroying life?" Lanko spread his hands. "We have here a fairly nice group of islands," he pointed out. "Not too spacious, of course, and not possessed of any luxurious cities. But there's water, and fresh fruits are available in plenty. The ships are provisioned fairly well, but they generally put in here for those very fruits. So, all we need do is give a little unwanted help."

"Shipwreck?"

"Something like that."

Banasel shook his head doubtfully. "It'll take a long time to undermine their reputation that way," he objected. "And we'd have a lot of people on these islands before we were through."

"I don't think so. Kondaro's a god, remember? And gods are infallible. Sira Nal can explain a few disappearances by accusations of irreverence, but he'll know better than to try explaining too many that way. I should imagine that the normal losses due to unexpected storms just about use up his allotment along that line."

Lanko shook his head. "No, Sira Nal's going to have to do something to prevent any rumor to the effect that the sea god is losing his grip." He paused. "And what ship do you think I spotted standing this way?"

"Oh, no! That's too much of a coincidence."

"No, not really. We took considerable time gathering in our boy here." Lanko inclined his head toward Genro Kir. "And the *Bordeklu's* home port is Tanagor, so Musa's old ship wouldn't spend too much of a layover in Kneuros. They're on schedule all right. You'd like to see your old friend, Dontor, again, wouldn't you, Musa? Sort of watch him try to save his ship in a real emergency?"

Musa grinned wolfishly. "Might be fun, at that," he agreed.

*****

Dontor strode firmly toward the ladder leading to the observation deck. The slaves had rigged the screen, and the priest looked proudly about this ship of which he was the actual and absolute master. Slowly, in majestic silence, he mounted the ladder and passed through the opening in the curtain.

He went to the middle of the forecastle, and stopped, waiting until the two junior priests had taken their positions near him and the slaves had set down the equipment chests.

The slaves straightened, and stood, arms folded, waiting. Dontor inspected the area, then moved his head imperiously.

"Very good," he said. "Take your posts."

As the slaves left, the three priests opened their instrument chests, removing navigational tools. Alnar went to the folding table, spread the chart over it, then took his watch out of the chest and stood back, holding it.

"Just about time, sir."

"Very well." Dontor glanced at the juniors, saw that Kuero had his sextant ready, and raised his own.

"Now," he instructed, when the readings were complete, "you will each calculate our position independently. I'll check your work when you have finished." He replaced his sextant in its case, then headed the small procession back to the cabins.

The ship's routine continued its uneventful course. The junior priests reported to Dontor with their calculations. Their work was examined, criticized, and finally approved. They were given further instructions. All was well aboard the *Bordeklu*.

The chief priest examined the charts and decided on the course for the next watch. The ship, he thought, would have to put in for water. And some of the island fruits would go well on the table. He set a course accordingly, and went topside to give instructions to the pilot.

*****

"Are you going to help them on their way?"

"It's not necessary, unless they start to by-pass the island. They'll have plenty to worry about when they try to anchor."

*****

Ahead of the ship, the sea was calm. No cloud marred the bright blue overhead. Slowly, a vague shape formed on the horizon, then it grew, to become a small, wooded island.

The ship continued on its course, approaching the bit of

land, and neared the breaker line. Orders sounded sharply, and the sails collapsed, spilling their wind. A crew forward cut the snubbing line, and the bow anchor splashed into the water.

The ship continued, and the anchor cable became taut. In defiance of the helmsman's efforts, the ship continued on a straight course. The bow line stretched, then loosened a little, as the anchor dragged. Still, the ship refused to swing. Hurriedly, the crew aft dropped the stern anchor. But the ship persisted on its course. All hands forward took shelter as the bow cable snapped and whipped viciously across the deck. The ship maintained its slow progress.

Frantically, the crew backed the sails, hoisting them to take all the wind possible. The helmsman spun the wheel in a final effort to turn the ship back to sea, then cast a glance astern at the taut cable, and ducked for shelter.

Sea anchors were hastily thrown overside, but still the ship approached the beach. The keel grated on sand, and the ship continued to move forward, as though, tired of the sea, it had decided to return to the forest. At last, wedged among the trees, the vessel stopped, far above the sands of the beach.

It was obviously there to stay.

Dontor stood, looking seaward. He shook his head, looked forward, then down at the ground beneath the ship. This was outside his experience. It was also outside the teaching so carefully instilled in his mind in the classrooms back at Tanagor, and later during those long days and nights when he was a junior priest. He had been taught to speak of sea demons, and to explain their actions, but he had not been told to believe in them.

He wondered if the great Kondaro really existed, and if he did, just what he might think of Dontor and of the ship he had so recently controlled. The thought crossed his mind that a real god might be somewhat critical of the priesthood of the sea.

"Something," he mused aloud, "will have to be done to

prevent loss of faith."

*****

"Well," remarked Lanko as he snapped the tractor off. "That's the first handful of sand for the cook pot."

*****

Sira Nal drummed impatiently on the table before him.

"I thought you could handle routine operations," he said bitingly. "Now, you tell me you've been missing ship after ship. What happened to them?"

The high priest shook his head. "We haven't been able to find out, sir."

"Do you mean to tell me you haven't anything to report on them?"

"We have sent out investigating ships, sir."

"And?"

"They haven't reported back, sir."

Sira Nal's checks paled slightly with rage as he stared at his underling.

"Miron," he snapped, "I'm not going to tell you exactly what to do, or how. You're supposed to know how to treat emergencies, not to call me any time something outside of routine happens. I want a report on those ships tomorrow morning." He glanced out of the window. "I don't care how you do it, but find out what happened, and I don't ever want to hear you admit again that you can't account for any ship I ask about. Is that clear?"

Miron nodded unhappily. "Yes, sir." He bowed and backed out of the room.

He forced himself to suppress his anger as he gently closed the door. Then, he stood for a moment, fists clenched, as he directed a furious gaze at the panels.

"How?" he thought. "How does he expect me to know what's going on at sea unless ships come in to give me information, or I am able to go out personally. And how does he expect me to make a personal check in one night?"

He started walking along the corridor. "I have no supernatural powers, and he knows it. He's the prophet.

60

Wish I'd never — "

He looked at the walls around him, then shook his head. No use thinking of that. None had ever successfully left the service of Kondaro. He continued to a stair, mounted it, then climbed ladders, to finally come out at the observation platform atop the temple. The observer bowed as his superior entered the little room just below the torch.

"Have there been any arrivals?"

"None, sir. I've seen no sails."

"I am going to send you an acolyte. If you see anything, send him to me immediately." Miron turned to go back to his quarters.

*****

After Miron's departure, Sira Nal sat for a time, still staring at the closed door. He had caught the wave of frustrated rage, and had almost responded for a second. But, he was forced to admit, the priest had justification. He had organized his forces adequately — had been a useful piece, within his limitations.

"I wonder," mused Sira Nal, "if Buron's pulling a sneak punch." He tilted his head. "It would be a little foul, but he might try something like that." He reviewed the rules they had agreed upon.

After all, this phase of his operation was outside of the home zone, and he was actually vulnerable to attack, even this early. He had assumed that Buron would be too busy developing his own pieces to spend any time on an offensive move at this stage. Of course, direct intervention was a little unethical, but Buron might try it.

He had thought his opponent would be too occupied to notice a move at this remote part of the board. And he had established this advance base by direct intervention, too. If Buron had noticed, and if he had checked Nal's methods, he might have felt justified, and have taken time for a quick, disruptive move. And Sira Nal was forced to admit that such a move might be allowed by Kir. It might be even approved, and hailed as a brilliant counter.

He rose to his feet, pacing about the room. If this were a move by Buron, the priesthood would be powerless to counter. It would take direct action by the player, of course. He grumbled to himself.

"Can't let this development be wasted. I'd lose too much time. I'll have to check personally."

He crossed to the window, opened it, and stepped out on the balcony.

Outside, the sun glinted on the harbor. A ship was standing out to sea, sails set to pick up the breeze from the headland. Sira Nal looked over toward the shipyards. It was a well organized secondary base, and it would probably develop into a highly valuable position. Somehow, he doubted that Buron would have been able to do as well, considering the time factor. He shook his head. This must be retained.

He threw the robe back, checked his equipment belt, adjusted his body shield, and stepped off the balcony, activating his levitation modulator. He swung around the outgoing ship, noting the activity aboard with approval, then headed seaward, to follow the route he had prescribed for his navigators. Somewhere out there, he would undoubtedly find Buron, poised to strike at any ship which bore the red and gold of Kondaro.

And when he did find him, he knew, he would have to outline a counter move which would force immunity to his sea lanes. He considered the possibilities as he sped over the sea.

*****

Musa sat before the detector, idly watching the vague patterns that grew and collapsed on the viewscreen. The scanner, Lanko had explained, picked up ghost images from heated air masses, or from clouds, but it discriminated against them, refusing to form a definite image unless a material body came within range. Then, it indicated range and azimuth, checked the body against the predetermined data, and the selective magnification circuits cut in.

62

As Musa watched, a sea bird appeared on the screen, outlined sharply against the darkness of the sea. The viewscreen tracked it for an instant, then continued its scan. Another body showed, seeming to come from under the sea. Musa looked at it curiously, then noticed that the range marks had tripped on. The screen was holding the object at center. A slight glow appeared, obscuring visual detail, and more marks showed in the legend. Musa turned around.

"Banasel," he called, "what's this?"

Banasel was engaged in his usual pastime of tinkering with the equipment. He looked around, then walked quickly over to the screen, to make adjustments. The object came into sharp focus, revealing itself as a man in the robes of Kondaro. Range and azimuth lines became clearly defined, and a graph showed in the legend space. Banasel glanced down at the dials.

"Hey, Lanko," he called, "we've got a customer."

"Where?" Lanko came out of the mess compartment.

"About seventy-one, true, and coming in fast. Range, about a hundred K's." Banasel twisted dials, watching the result on the screen. "Looks as though our friend's coming in for a conference."

"Screens?"

"Personal body shield. Probably a Morei twelve. Nothing special."

Lanko got into the gunner's chair and punched a button. The sight screen lit, showing the approaching body clearly. He turned a knob, increasing magnification.

"All dressed up in his ceremonial robes, too," he laughed. "This kid could have done well as a clothing designer."

He adjusted a few knobs, examining a meter. Then, he reached for the weapon's grip.

"No point in discussing matters with him now. He can talk after we get him in, and he's just about in range now." He brought the hair-lines on the viewscreen to center on the approaching figure, and squeezed the grip.

*****

Sira Nal felt the sudden pressure. Annoyed, he reached to his belt, to turn his shield to full power. This was highly unethical. Buron should certainly know better than to resort to personal attack. Such action could be protested, and Sira Nal could demand concessions.

He looked ahead, searchingly. The horizon ahead was broken by a faint cloud, which indicated the islands, but there was no evidence of his opponent. He shook his head, and started to rise, but his shield was failing. Suddenly, he became aware of the overheating generator pack. Something was decidedly wrong. He reached for his own hand weapon, still searching for his attacker. At last, he noticed a slight shimmer, dead ahead. He pointed the weapon.

"Now, now," cautioned a voice, "you could get hurt that way. Close down your shield and relax. This is a guard flier. You're in arrest tractor."

Sira Nal recognized that the tractor was pulling him ahead. His generator pack was heating up dangerously.

He was being captured!

Furiously, he thought of the attacks he had made in similar manner, in this same area. He still could remember the horrified expression on one shipowner's face just before his ship broke to bits under him.

They wouldn't get him, though.

They couldn't.

He would blast them out of his path. Just as he had blasted the presumptuous natives who opposed him.

Thumbing the hand weapon to full blast, he centered it on the faint shimmer ahead, and squeezed the trigger.

Let the meddlers look out for themselves.

*****

Banasel winced a little as the fireball spread, then rose skyward, to form a large cloud.

"You could have relaxed," he protested. "The blast wouldn't have jolted our screen too much, and you could have gotten him again."

"I know." Lanko flicked off the gunnery switches and leaned back, rubbing his head. "There was a possibility, and I fully intended to relax. But the decision time was short, and frankly, those thoughts of his overrode me for just too long. That boy was dangerous!"

He turned to Genro Kir, who was looking with horrified fascination at the still growing cloud in the screen.

"It's unfortunate. We'll try to get your other partner alive."

"You destroyed him!" Kir looked a little sick.

"No. We didn't destroy him. He should have known better than to fire into a tractor. I'll have to admit, I did slip a little. I assumed he was the usual type of drone. I didn't recognize the full extent of his aberration."

Lanko got out of his chair, and crossed the room, to confront the prisoner.

"Look, Kir. I don't know whether your other partner's like that one or not. But I think it's about time you helped a little. If you had given us clues to Sira Nal's personality and probable location, we might have been able to take precautions. He might be with us now. Or, do you enjoy seeing your friends turn themselves into flaming clouds of smoke?"

"You mean I ... I'm responsible ... for that?"

"Partially. You helped them. You refused any assistance in their capture. And you knew they were going to be captured, one way or another."

Kir directed a horrified look at the screen.

"What can I do?"

"Get in contact with Koree Buron. Tell him what happened here. Tell him, too, that we're looking for him, and that there is a Sector Guardsman due to join us within a few hours. Explain to him that there will be direction-finders on him very soon, and that any effort he may make to use his body shield, his weapons, or even his thought-radiations, will be noted, and will lead to him.

"Once you establish contact, we will ride in, if you wish. And we can assure him that he'll be either hunted down promptly, or he will have to assume and accept the role of a native — and a very inconspicuous, uninfluential native, at that.

"Tell him that he is free to come to us and surrender at any time within the next twenty hours, planetary. After that, he will be taken by the most expedient means. After the surrender deadline, you can assure him that his life will be of less importance to us, and to the Sector Guardsman, than that of the most humble native.

"Here's your mental amplifier, if you need it."

Genro Kir looked at the proffered circlet, then slowly extended a hand. He took the device, turned it around in his hands for a few moments, then put it on.

Suddenly, his face set in decision, and he sat quietly for a while, grim faced. At last, he looked up.

"I got him. He argued a little, but he had a poor argument, and he knew it. He'll be here within an hour, screens down."

THE END

www.ingramcontent.com/pod-product-compliance
Lightning Source LLC
Chambersburg PA
CBHW020649130626
46552CB00003B/1458